For my sisters, with love ~ S.R.
For Jonny and Katie ~ S.A.L.

MYRIAD BOOKS LIMITED
35 Bishopsthorpe Road, London SE26 4PA

First published in 2000 by
FRANCES LINCOLN LIMITED
4 Torriano Mews, Torriano Avenue
London NW5 2RZ

ISBN 1 84746 009 7

EAN 9 781 84746 009 7

Printed in China

'SIMON SAYS!'

Shen Roddie  Sally Anne Lambert

MYRIAD BOOKS LIMITED

Simon Pig was digging in his garden
when along came Sally Goose, on her way
to the Giant Melon Fair.

"Ooh! Ouch! This is hard work!"
grumbled Simon.
"Why don't you make a game of it?"
asked Sally Goose. "Then it will be fun!"

"Good idea!" cried Simon. "Let's play Simon Says!
You do whatever Simon Says. But when I say
'Sally Says', you must stand still.
If you don't, you're out!" said Simon.
"That's easy!" said Sally Goose.

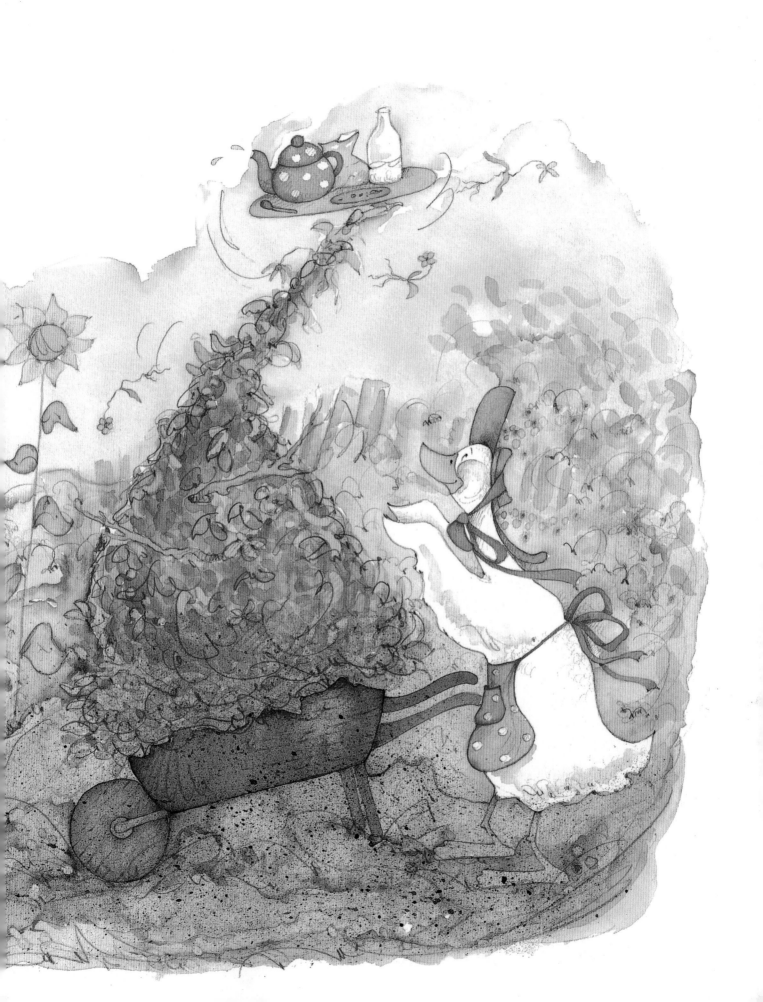

So Simon said:

"Simon Says dig a hole and plant a carrot!"

Sally dug a hole and planted a carrot.
She was very pleased.

"Great game!" said Sally Goose.

"Simon Says make a scarecrow
and stick him in!"

Sally made a flappity scarecrow
and stuck him in.
"This is fun!" she said.

"Simon Says go upstairs and run the bath!"

Sally ran into the house and up the stairs.

She turned on the tap and ran Simon a bubbly bath.

"Simon Says scrub my back and clip my nails!"
said Simon.

"Ugh! What a dirty pig," Sally thought,
as she scrubbed and clipped.

"Simon Says wash the dishes and stack them up!"
Sally washed a whole week's dishes and stacked
them all up.

"This game is tiring me out!" said Sally Goose.
"Can I have a cup of tea now?"
"No. You don't want tea," said Simon.
"You're doing very well. Keep it up."

Simon carried on:

"Simon Says bake a cake and make a jelly."

Sally Goose groaned.
She baked a cake...

and made a jelly.

"When are you going to say 'Sally Says'?"
asked Sally. "I need a break!"

"Can't tell you, can I?" said Simon.
"I need to catch you out!"

"Well, you won't," thought Sally.
"I'm not such a silly goose. I won't be caught out.
You'll see!"

"Simon Says make me a wig and sew me a waistcoat."

Sally made him a wig and sewed him a waistcoat.

"Aren't I gorgeous!" said Simon, admiring himself
in the mirror.

"Not a bit, bully Pig!" said Sally, half collapsing
on the floor.

"Simon Says knit me a hammock and swing
me to sleep!"

Sally knitted a knobbly hammock and swung
him to sleep.

"Hurray!" said Sally when Simon began to snore.
"I'm off!"

But just as Sally shut the gate, Simon jumped up and said, "Sally says leave the garden and shut the gate! There!" said Simon. "You've left the garden and shut the gate! You've done what Sally Says. You're not supposed to do that! You should be standing still!"

"You're out, Sally Goose!" yelled Simon.
"I'm not playing!" Sally yelled back.
"Not unless I have a go!"
"Oh, all right, then," said Simon.
"You can have a go. But only one
or you'll be late for your fair!"

Sally Goose smiled.

"Well then," said Sally Goose. "Simon Says give Sally and her melon a piggyride all the way to the fair!

And make it QUICK..."

And Simon did!